When Sleeping Dogs Awaken

Anne Schraff

SADDLEBACK PAGETURNERS

• MYSTERY •

PAGETURNERS

ADVENTURE

MYSTERY

Development and Production: Laurel Associates, Inc.
Cover Illustrator: Black Eagle Productions

SADDLEBACK
PUBLISHING · INC.
Three Watson
Irvine, CA 92618-2767

E-Mail: info@sdlback.com
Website: www.sdlback.com

ISBN 1-56254-180-3

Printed in the United States of America
05 04 03 02 01 00   9 8 7 6 5 4 3 2 1

CONTENTS

Chapter 1

Tanner Brice liked the tiny room he'd made for himself. It was on the sunporch of his mom and stepdad's apartment. The room was important to him. He'd rather have a cubbyhole that was *all* his than share a nice bedroom with his half-brother, Damon. Damon was 14—a real jerk in Tanner's eyes.

Tanner was 21, and he was just finishing up a two-year automotive repair course at the community college. He also worked at a quickie lube place. After Tanner got his certificate, he'd be on his own. Then he'd find an apartment as soon as he could. He was really looking forward to that. Tanner's stepdad got on his nerves, and Damon wasn't much better.

Tanner's biological father was killed by a hit-and-run driver when Tanner was just five. Mom didn't waste any time in marrying Floyd Richards. He was a salesman who peddled stupid products like food supplements or magic cleaning solutions. Tanner looked at him as sort of a modern snake-oil salesman.

Damon was born of that marriage. Maybe that was why Tanner didn't feel much connected to his half-brother. Damon was too much like old Floyd. He even *looked* like him. Floyd and Damon were both stocky, pudgy guys. Tanner was tall and lean like his father.

Tanner kept a photograph of his dad on his dresser. He was a handsome man with intense brown eyes, a squarish jaw, and a manly smile. He looked like the sort of man Tanner wanted to be someday—solid, dependable, strong, with a great personality.

Floyd Richards was a squat little joker with a high, excitable voice. He annoyed Tanner. It was embarrassing how Floyd always tried to rope in the neighbors with one of his stupid business scams. He was in on pyramid schemes to grow hair on bald men, and magic food supplements that were supposed to restore youth and ward off all the diseases known to man. Tanner called Floyd the "flim-flam man" behind his back.

Guys that Tanner went to school with were always stopping him and saying, "Hey, man, that junk your dad sold my mom for taking spots out of clothes doesn't work."

"He's not my dad," Tanner would always say. But it didn't do much good. The smell of Floyd's fishy deals seemed to stick to Tanner anyway.

Tanner was getting ready to go to class when he heard his mom and stepdad talking in the bedroom.

"Hey, baby, you look beee-yoot-iful this morning," Floyd was saying. It

7

made Tanner feel sick. He was always sort of angry at his mother for marrying a guy like Floyd. How could she have settled for a flim-flam man when she had once had a guy like Dad? What had happened to her standards?

"Come on, Floyd," Mom giggled. "I gotta get dressed and go to work." She was a checker at the local supermarket. She brought in more solid money than all of Floyd's schemes put together.

"Baby, I can't get enough of you," Floyd said in his stupid voice.

Tanner wanted to throw up. His father had been killed one December, right after Christmas. Mom had married Floyd the following September. So *soon*—like only nine months later.

"Floyd Richards, you get out of here and let a girl get dressed," Mom scolded in a laughing voice. Mom was very good looking. Tanner thought his mother was just about the most beautiful lady in the whole darn neighborhood. When he and his mother would go somewhere, people often thought she was Tanner's older sister. He was proud of having a mom who looked so good. Now Mom giggled, "Oh, for goodness sake, Floyd, you've known me for 18 years now! Don't tell me I still get you all that excited!"

Tanner stiffened. *Eighteen years?* That wasn't the story Mom had always told him. She said she'd met Floyd when he was in life insurance. He'd helped her straighten out Dad's policies. Mom always said Floyd's kindness to the new widow was what started them dating. What was this 18 years all about?

Did Mom know Floyd while Dad was still living? Dad had died 16 years ago. Did she know Floyd *two years* before that? A spark of rage began to flicker inside Tanner. What was going on? What *had been* going on?

"Hey, Damon," Mom called into the kitchen. "Get a move on! Finish your breakfast and get ready for school. You don't want to be late again, do you?"

"Yeah," Floyd chimed in. "These days they lock you out of your classes when you're late, don't they?"

"It wouldn't be so bad to get locked out of history," Damon said, slipping on his backpack and heading out the door. Floyd left then, too. There was nobody in the kitchen now but Tanner and his mother.

"Mom," Tanner said, "I was just wondering about something. How long did you know Floyd before you guys got married?"

Mom put down her coffee cup and stared at Tanner. "Now where did *that* question come from? After all these years, what difference does it make? I told you he was the insurance man who helped me get the settlement on your dad's policy. He felt sorry for how sad I was, and he took me out to dinner. Then I guess we just fell in love. But you've heard all that before, Tanner."

"Yeah, Mom, but a few minutes ago I overheard you saying that you and Floyd have known each other for 18 years," Tanner said suspiciously. "But 18 years ago Dad was still here. I mean, did you guys know each other *before* Dad was killed or something?"

Like angry hornets, irrational suspicions buzzed in Tanner's mind. Old Floyd was a loser. *Of course* he would be real anxious to move in on a lady in a nice apartment. Especially one who owned a late-model car and had some fine blue-chip stocks building up.

"Oh, Tanner," Mom laughed, "I guess I misspoke myself is all. What on earth is sticking in your craw, boy?"

Tanner could swear that Mom was lying about something. She had that funny look on her face. Something was wrong, and she was hiding it. Maybe she'd been hiding it for 18 years.

Maybe it was something nasty.

Chapter 2

"Mom, you *sure* you didn't know Floyd before Dad died?" Tanner repeated the question.

"Tanner, I don't much appreciate being grilled by my son at eight o'clock in the morning. Why are you so curious about stuff that happened almost 20 years ago? Will you quit it? Floyd and I have been married almost 16 years— we've got a happy family here. *What is your problem?* Can't you just let sleeping dogs lie?" Now Mom sounded not only guilty, but angry.

Tanner let it drop. He shouldered his own backpack and headed for his little pickup truck. He was doing very well at his classes in school. His instructors told him he had a real knack for fixing cars.

There was good money to be made by skilled auto mechanics.

As Tanner drove toward college, he passed the spot where his father had died 16 years ago. Tanner still had all the newspaper clippings about the accident. He had gone down to the library when he was a freshman in high school and made copies of all the stories. It was such a terrible accident that the paper had made quite a lot of it.

Mack Brice had been a bright young accountant, married with a young son. He worked downtown. But because parking was such a problem, he took the bus and trolley to work. He was standing at the bus stop one day when an out-of-control car ran up on the sidewalk. The young man was crushed to death against the brick building on the corner. The driver had then thrown his car in reverse, backed up off the sidewalk, and sped on down the street.

Although several witnesses gave

good descriptions of the car, that vehicle bore no license plates and was never found. All the onlookers knew of the driver was that it was a man. Neither car nor driver was ever found.

It was almost as if the hit and run driver had aimed for the sidewalk and *deliberately* killed Mack Brice before speeding off. It was almost as if it *wasn't* an accident at all.

But that was crazy thinking, wasn't it? Whenever Tanner thought about the accident, he'd remind himself that it was nothing but crazy to think his dad had been murdered. Who would want to murder a nice young accountant with a wife and little kid? It didn't make any sense, so Tanner would always stifle his suspicion and forget it—for a while.

But now, this morning, a horrible new possibility came to mind. It was so awful, so *repulsive*, that Tanner had trouble focusing on it. But what if there was something to it after all?

What if Floyd Richards was sweet-talking Mom even *before* Dad died? What if they had a little flirtation going? Nothing serious. Maybe just jokes shared, compliments exchanged. What if Floyd had seen his chance then? What if he saw his big opportunity to move in on another man's little paradise? A beautiful wife who made good money, a family with a stock portfolio already earning interest. . . . What if Floyd had thought it would be no big deal to arrange an accident and move right in on Mack Brice's sweet life?

Sitting at the wheel of his pickup, Tanner broke into a cold sweat. No, he told himself, Floyd was a flim-flam man for sure—but *murder* was a wild reach. Even Floyd wasn't the kind of snake who'd kill a good man just to get his wife. It was too off the wall. . . .

"What's the matter with you, man?" Tanner scolded himself. "You're grasping at straws. Just because you don't like the guy is hardly a reason to think he's a murderer. Just because he annoys you with his weird ways is no cause for getting paranoid. . . ."

Tanner gripped the steering wheel and tried to push all his suspicions out of his mind. They were all nonsense, he told himself, just the figments of his own fevered imagination.

In another few months Tanner's whole life would be great. He'd have his own apartment, and he'd be bringing in good money as a mechanic. And to top if all off, there was Bianca. Tanner had met Bianca in his senior year in high school, and they had been dating ever since. She was a tall, willowy girl with big doe eyes. She was learning to be a medical records clerk in the same college that Tanner attended. Every day Tanner and Bianca met for lunch to talk about their future. They were planning to marry in about a year.

Tanner loved Bianca. She was the

greatest girl he'd ever met. Tanner had met her parents and got along fine with them. He liked Bianca's sisters, her whole family. But whenever Bianca hinted that she'd like to meet Tanner's family, he had made up excuses. Tanner was ashamed of Floyd Richards and his goofy son Damon. He flat out didn't want Bianca to meet them.

Once, when Tanner and Bianca were eating lunch, Bianca had joked, "Tanner, you're not a child of aliens, are you? Sometimes I think you were dropped off of a spaceship and that's why you can't introduce me to your parents." She had laughed when she had said that, but she wasn't really joking. Tanner could always tell the level of her seriousness from her eyes.

"You'll meet them, baby," Tanner promised. "Of course my dad is dead. But I've got some great pictures of him and me from when I was little."

"Yeah, you told me that," Bianca

said, "but I'd love to meet your mom. Your mother must be a real special lady to have raised a guy like you."

"Oh, yeah, she is," Tanner said, "but my stepdad is sort of a jerk. And my half-brother is a weirdo ... I don't get along too good with either of them."

"That's no reason for me not to meet them," Bianca said softly. "Maybe I'd like your stepdad and your brother. I've had some cool jerks for friends."

"Yeah, well, pretty soon," Tanner promised.

Now, as Tanner pulled into the community college parking lot, he got to thinking of his dad again. He didn't remember much from when he was two or three, but he had a lot of memories after he turned four. Dad had taken him out to baseball games and to the park. Sometimes they went to amusement parks together, too.

Tanner tried to remember times when the whole family had gone along on those outings. But suddenly he realized that Mom hadn't usually come with them. Tanner remembered riding on his tall dad's shoulders and getting a yellow chin from eating hotdogs with mustard on them.

But why wasn't Mom along?

Were his parents having trouble in their marriage? Were they estranged? Was Mom secretly hanging out with Floyd even then?

The suspicion had been planted. Mom's remark about knowing Floyd for 18 years was growing like a poisonous weed in Tanner's brain. Once more he broke into a cold sweat.

Something terrible had happened to his beloved father, and that was hard enough to take. But if it wasn't an accident, it must have been murder. And Tanner couldn't live with that. He just *couldn't*.

Chapter 3

After classes that afternoon, Tanner decided not to go straight home. He wasn't working at the lube shop until tomorrow, so he had some time to kill. He drove to Grandma's little apartment near downtown. Grandma Brice was very special to him. She was his only living link to his dad. Tanner made sure to visit her frequently.

Grandma Brice was a tall, strong woman of 75 who had raised three fine sons and a daughter with her husband. After his death, she'd spent most of her time doing charity work. She was always bringing hot meals to the sick and housebound, still driving her 25-year-old Ford. Grandma Brice had a lovely soprano voice, and she led the singing in the Sweet Sounds of Heaven chorus at her church.

"Why, Tanner, what a nice surprise!" she said when she saw him. "Child, you are so handsome I could eat you up! Usually you come to see me on Sunday, and here it is only Wednesday. How did you know I just took a pecan pie out of the oven?"

Tanner sat with his grandmother, eating pecan pie and drinking coffee. He told her about his college classes, and all about Bianca. Grandma Brice was the only relative Tanner really shared his life with. He didn't even tell Mom much about his plans or about Bianca. He loved his mother, but it was sort of like he had a grudge against her. One way of getting back at her for marrying Floyd was to withhold secrets from her, to shut her out of his life.

"You know what, Grandma? I feel real bad that they never caught the driver who killed Dad," Tanner said suddenly.

Grandma looked surprised. "Why, Tanner, you haven't mentioned that in such a long time. I thought you had put it behind you, made your peace with it. Child, that's *such* a long time ago now! We've already done our grieving over your dad, haven't we? I still visit Macky's grave every holiday and put flowers there—but his soul has ridden off on the wings of angels, and he's been safely home for a good long while. Let the good Lord deal with the man who killed him," Grandma said.

"But I can't help thinking about it, Grandma. What if it *wasn't* an accident at all? What if the guy deliberately drove up on that sidewalk and killed Dad?" Tanner insisted.

"Oh, honey," Grandma said, patting Tanner's hand, "don't brood on such things. You'll only make yourself sick."

"Grandma . . . uh . . . Mom and Dad . . . they were happy, weren't they? I mean a long time ago, when I was little. They were real happy, weren't they?" Tanner asked. "I *need* to know."

A sad, clouded look came into Grandma's eyes. "Child, why are you dredging all this up now?" she asked in a worried voice.

"I don't know. I really don't like my stepdad, you know. I told you he's always selling people junk that isn't any good—stuff that doesn't do what it's supposed to do. Stupid colored pills that are supposed to make old people young, and all kinds of scam-type things. That stuff cheats people. I think he's a crook," Tanner said.

"Oh, Tanner, I'm sure he's not that bad. If he was really cheating people, he'd be in jail. A lot of products they advertise on TV aren't much good, either. That's just how things are these days," Grandma said.

It dawned on Tanner then that Grandma had not answered his question about Mom and Dad being happy.

"Grandma—Mom and Dad, they got along, right?" he asked again.

"They had their ups and downs like everybody else. People aren't perfect, honey. And *all* of us bring our mixed-up selves into a marriage and that causes a lot of strife," Grandma said.

"Dad was always great, though," Tanner said. "I remember him taking me to baseball games. It was really fun being with Dad. If he had lived, I know we'd be best buddies now. Man, we would've gotten along so great! But I don't remember Mom coming with us many times. I wonder why that was. . . ."

Tanner was fishing for something, any little scrap of information. He knew Grandma Brice would never come right out and say her daughter-in-law was cheating on her son, but maybe she'd drop a clue.

"Well, your mother didn't like sports, and Macky was crazy about *any* sport. All my boys loved sports. You know, my eldest son, your Uncle Ben, he coaches a football team down south. Mack was a lot like his brother. Those boys just *loved* sports. . . ." Grandma said wistfully.

"Something Mom said kinda worried me, Grandma. This morning she said that she had known Floyd for 18 years. Before now, she's always said she met Floyd Richards *after* Dad died. Then today I heard her telling Floyd how they'd known each other for 18 years now. That'd mean she knew him while Dad was still alive," Tanner said.

Grandma grew pale. "What are you saying, child?" she asked.

"I don't know. I was just wondering if maybe Mom was, you know—sorta hanging out with Floyd before Dad was . . . killed," Tanner said. He didn't really expect that his grandmother would tell him, even if that was true. Grandma Brice was a very decent, religious woman. She never gossiped. She had to know that revealing such a dark secret would ruin Tanner's relationship with the only parent he had left, his mom. But maybe she'd say *something* to clear things up.

"Tanner, your mother has always been a righteous woman," Grandma Brice said in a trembling voice. "You must never even *think* such a thing of your mother. She probably knew Floyd on a purely business basis. Maybe she bought an insurance policy from him or something—but there was nothing more than that while she was married to Mack."

"Yeah, you must be right," Tanner said. "I shouldn't even question Mom." Then he gave his grandma a hug. "I didn't mean to upset you. I love you, Grandma."

As Tanner was driving home, he wondered why Grandma had gotten so upset. Was it because Tanner was getting nearer to the truth, or because what he said was so far from the truth?

But how would Grandma know? If Floyd Richards had had anything to do with Dad's death, Grandma wouldn't know a thing about it. She would never cover up for her son's murderer. If Floyd was mixed up in something that evil, he had fooled Grandma Brice, too.

Tanner made up his mind to get to the bottom of it, no matter what. The seeds of suspicion had been planted this morning. Now his dislike of Floyd was watering the growing plant. Tanner had to find out what had *really* happened. Then he could either nail Floyd once and for all, or let his dead father rest in peace.

# Chapter 4

When Tanner got home, the door to his little makeshift bedroom was open. Damon was in there, rummaging around. Tanner flew into an instant rage. "Hey, you little creep, get outta my room!" Tanner shouted.

"Keep your shirt on, man," Damon said. "I just thought maybe you had an extra cartridge—"

Tanner grabbed Damon's shoulders and gave him a violent shove out of the room. "I don't want you messing with my stuff, okay? This is *my* room and you don't come in here and just help yourself to my stuff, man!" Tanner yelled.

"Hey, don't have a cow, man," Damon shouted back. "You're such a selfish weirdo I can't believe it. I guess you must take after your old man. I hear he was a hothead, too."

Tanner's fury went up a notch after the insult to his father. There were no adults at home to put a damper on the argument, so Tanner gave full vent to his rage. He grabbed Damon's shoulders again and rammed him against the hallway wall.

"What do *you* know about my father, you little cockroach? I'll tell you what you know—*nothing*! When he died, you weren't even born yet. My dad was the best guy who ever lived. You're not fit to walk in his shadow," Tanner shouted in Damon's face.

Damon sneered, "Ha! My friend at school, Tommy Benson, he said his dad and your dad went to school together. Tommy's father said Mack Brice was a hotheaded punk," Damon said.

Tanner flinched. "You take that back," he screamed. He started to shake

Damon like a cat shakes a mouse.

Just then, Mom came in the door. "Tanner! Damon! Stop it!" Mom screamed, drawn to the hallway by the thumps and shouting. "Stop that fighting right now! You should be ashamed of yourselves."

Damon turned to his mother. "Don't yell at *me*, Mom. He started it! He went ballistic just 'cause I went in his room to see if he had an extra cartridge for my word processor," he said.

"The little scorpion has no business going in my room and poking around in my stuff," Tanner cried.

Mom glared at Tanner. "You are way out of bounds, young man," she said sharply. "You should know better. You're a man now—a full grown man— bullying a 15-year-old kid. A *man* doesn't act like you're acting, Tanner. I'm ashamed of you."

All the bitterness Tanner had felt over the years bubbled up inside him like hot lava coming to the surface of a volcano. He resented Mom's marriage to Floyd Richards. He resented Damon coming along and being fawned over as the precious, adorable baby, the cute little pudgy kid.

"If you can't behave yourself like a man, you're not welcome in this house, Tanner!" Mom shouted. She had lost her cool, too. She hadn't meant to say something that harsh. The minute she had said it, she regretted it—but the words were out there now, hanging between mother and son like a sword.

"I was *never* really welcome in this house after my father died," Tanner cried out bitterly. "When you married that little jerk—"

"Don't you call your stepfather a jerk!" Mom cut in sharply.

Tanner finished his sentence grimly, because he knew bridges were being burned. But at the moment he didn't care. "When you married Floyd

Richards, the two of you and Damon got to be a family, and I got shut out big time!"

"Tanner, that's not true and you know it," Mom said, starting to cry. "Floyd tried in every way he knew to be a father to you. And heaven knows I've loved you as much as any mother can love a child!"

"When my dad was killed there wasn't anything here for me anymore," Tanner said. He went in his room and slammed the door behind him. He was shaking with anger. But he didn't do what he usually did after family arguments—sit on the bed and sulk until it was time for dinner.

This time Tanner started packing. He threw his possessions into two suitcases. There wasn't much. Jeans, t-shirts, one good pair of slacks, a good blue shirt, and the dress shoes he had worn at graduation. Then he squeezed in his father's pictures, some pennants from his favorite baseball team, and a picture of Grandma Brice. His running shoes and binders from college took up the rest of the space in the second suitcase.

When Tanner opened the door, he had a suitcase in each hand. But Floyd Richards blocked his path.

"Where do you think you're going?" Floyd demanded.

Chapter 5

"I'm outta here!" Tanner shot back.

"You've upset your mother very much, boy. You better just unpack that stuff and go talk to her," Floyd said.

"I'm moving out, man. I don't want to live here anymore, so get out of my way," Tanner said, dodging past his stepdad.

"Get a grip on yourself, Tanner. You're just letting a silly tantrum get the best of you. Don't do something you'll regret," Floyd said, following Tanner down the hall.

Tanner stopped and looked back at his stepfather. "Look, I know what happened 18 years ago, okay? I figured it all out—and it makes me sick to my stomach. I don't want to look at your face anymore, man."

Floyd stepped back, stunned. His jaw dropped. His eyes looked like they might pop out of his head. It was just the reaction Tanner needed to convince him that he was onto something. The two of them, Mom and Floyd, *had* cheated on Dad. Whatever else might have happened, Tanner wasn't sure. But he would find out. Next he was going to pore over all the details of the accident to see if the cops had let some important clue slip by them.

Tanner went out the door and then down the steps, lugging his two suitcases. He figured that Mom and Floyd had their heads together about now. They were racking their brains trying to figure out how much Tanner knew. Maybe they were scared. At least Floyd was. And Mom loved Floyd. For some reason she really loved him. Tanner had always seen that—and it *disgusted* him. Sometimes it enraged him. How could Mom love such a pudgy little weasel who made his money on ripoff schemes?

Tanner had a friend from the lube shop, Rod Withers, who lived in a boarding house near the college. Rod was always asking Tanner to room with him and split expenses. He had a big room with twin beds. The landlady there was real nice. She often invited her tenants, mostly college kids, to free meals. Tanner figured if he split expenses with Rod, he could handle it. It wouldn't be as cheap as living at home, but not seeing Floyd and Damon every day was worth the extra cost.

"Hey, you finally took the big step, huh?" Rod asked with a grin when Tanner appeared with his suitcases. "You're way overdue, man. Come on in and stash your stuff."

Tanner unloaded his few possessions into a small dresser. Rod gave him half the closet, which was plenty. Then Rod and Tanner went down the street to the coffee shop that was a favorite student hangout.

As they sat drinking black coffee, Tanner confided his suspicions about Floyd Richards to Rod. He had already told Rod how much he disliked his stepfather, but now he shared his doubts about his father's death.

"Man, that's scary," Rod said. "But I guess it happens more than we think. A marriage turns sour and maybe the lady looks for greener pastures. If some sweet-talking dude comes along, who knows what could happen? If he has to knock off the husband, so what?"

"I've got no proof or anything," Tanner said, "but I'm sure of one thing. If Floyd had something to do with Dad's death, Mom wouldn't have known anything about it. I'm going to try to see the accident report. Maybe some of the witnesses who saw the accident are still alive. I might just turn up something, you know?"

"Man," Rod said, "wouldn't it be something if you solved a 16-year-old murder case?"

"Well, I'm not saying it *was* murder. It might have been an accident. But it's real strange that this guy would drive up on a sidewalk, kill my dad, and then speed away. It doesn't sound right. If the guy's car was out of control, wouldn't he have tried to find help for his victim?" Tanner said.

"Sounds like you may be onto something, bro," Rod said.

At school the next day, Tanner told Bianca that he had moved out of his house. "It's time I was on my own," Tanner said, not wanting to go into the details of the bitter argument. "The only way I'm gonna get responsible is to take control of my own life."

"I guess so," Bianca said. "Your folks must be proud of you for having the courage to make the big step."

Tanner didn't answer. He didn't want

to go down that road with Bianca. He didn't want to shock her with such a terrible suspicion before he was sure about what really happened. Right now he was running mostly on rage and vague suspicion. He *wanted* to believe that Floyd Richards was an evil man. Tanner was no fool. He *knew* that wanting it so badly might cloud his thought processes. So he couldn't go off half-cocked. He had to go through the circumstances of the accident carefully and thoroughly, without prejudice.

At the police station, Tanner read the accident report. Then he went to the library to look for any articles in other papers that he might have missed. He found out the year and make of the death car. He found the names of three witnesses. For the first time, he learned that his father had not been killed instantly. The poor man had lived for five hours, and then died from massive internal bleeding at the hospital.

According to one newspaper report, Mack Brice had been conscious when the first witness arrived. That witness said that Tanner's dad didn't seem to be seriously hurt. He could only say that the car had sped away, and that he had seen Mack Brice crumpled against the wall. Nobody had actually witnessed the accident itself.

Two of the witnesses had died in the 16 years since the accident. The one who remained alive still lived in the neighborhood. He had run a barber shop on the corner where Tanner's dad died. Now he was retired, but he was still living in the apartment over the barber shop, which was now run by his son.

After school, Tanner drove there to see the man.

"My name is Tanner Brice," he told the elderly man at the door. "About 16 years ago, you were one of the witnesses who saw my dad get hit and killed. I wonder if you'd be willing to talk to me about the accident for a few minutes."

"Sure, come on in," said the old man. "Time I got plenty of."

Tanner sat down in the apartment and accepted a cup of coffee from Mr. Hy Rothstein. "I remember your father. He was such a fine, clean-cut man—and so *young*! What a tragedy!" he said sadly. "You resemble him, son. You are a fine-looking young man, too."

"Could you tell me anything about the car that hit him?" Tanner asked.

"Just that it was a blue car. It was already driving away when I saw it," Rothstein explained.

"Did you see the driver at all?" Tanner asked.

"Just a fleeting glimpse. That's what I told the police. I did see the man's arm. I noticed that it was pudgy. He was resting his arm on the open car window. I remember thinking he looked *relaxed*. He was just sitting there like he was on a nice drive—and here he was leaving

41

behind a man he had killed! It seemed cold . . . *very* cold."

Pudgy? That word stuck in Tanner's mind. *Pudgy*. Like Floyd Richards . . . but the world was full of overweight men.

Tanner thanked the retired barber and left. As he was driving home from class the next day, he felt frustrated. He didn't know where to turn to get more information. Then he remembered the guy his dad used to work for, Bob Sorenson. The company was a financial advice service, and Dad was an accountant there. Sorenson had always said Dad was the best employee he'd ever had.

Tanner remembered his father taking him to the golf course one day while Dad and Sorenson played a few rounds. They seemed to be more than just boss and employee. They were like friends. Tanner remembered how they had laughed together.

Tanner's heart raced. Maybe Sorenson would know something about what had been going on then. If he and Dad were best friends, maybe Dad had mentioned marital problems. Maybe Dad even told Sorenson that Mom had a slimy friend named Floyd Richards. Dad wouldn't have told just *any* old boss about his personal problems, of course. But once Dad had told Tanner that Sorenson was "the best boss in the whole world," and that they were buddies. They even went on fishing trips together.

"Yeah," Tanner told Rod, "it's worth a try talking to that guy."

"Man," Rod said with a worried look on his face, "you really got a tiger by the tail here. Just don't get *obsessed*, okay?"

# Chapter 6

Tanner called Mr. Sorenson's office and asked for an appointment. He explained that he was Mack Brice's son, and he had serious doubts about his father's death being an accident. Mr. Sorenson gave Tanner an appointment for 3:00 P.M. the next day.

The financial services firm was high up on the eleventh floor of a downtown building that appeared to be made entirely of glass. When Tanner walked into the reception area, he almost sank to his ankles in the deep pile of the expensive rug. Tanner figured the people who came here for financial advice had to be the super rich.

Bob Sorenson was even more friendly than Tanner had expected. He invited

Tanner into his private office and extended his hand in a warm handshake. "Tanner, I can't tell you how much your dad meant to me. It really threw me for a loop when you said on the phone that you think his death might not have been an accident. I'm telling you, when Mack Brice was killed, it was like I had not only lost my best friend, but my right arm here in the business. I was on the verge of offering him a partnership. He was *that* valuable around here," he said.

Tanner sat in one of the big leather chairs opposite Sorenson's desk. "I kinda wonder if Dad was killed on purpose. It seemed like the guy might have hit him deliberately. I don't have a lot of money, but I'm thinking about maybe hiring a private detective to look into it. But first I was kind of wondering if you have any information that I don't have," Tanner explained.

"You may be right, Tanner. It always seemed to me that there was something fishy about the accident. When a car accidentally hits somebody, it doesn't usually get away without being seen. Of course the police eventually decided it *was* an accident. . . ." Sorenson said, his voice trailing off.

"Yeah, but they never found the guy who hit Dad. Never found the car, either. How come the car wasn't found? Cars don't just *vanish*—not unless somebody is trying real hard to cover up something. Maybe it was a murder from the git-go. Maybe the car was hustled off according to a plan," Tanner said.

"I see what you mean," Sorenson said thoughtfully.

"Uh . . . one reason I came here, Mr. Sorenson, I was wondering if Dad ever talked to you about, you know . . . personal stuff. Did he ever tell you something that would explain why somebody wanted to kill him?" Tanner asked. "Like personal problems. . . ."

"Problems of what kind, Tanner?"

Sorenson asked with a curious look.

"Well, like my mom got married to this creepy guy just a few months after Dad died. I'm thinking maybe my stepdad knew Mom like a long time before the . . . uh . . . accident. Maybe it was real convenient for him that Dad was out of the way," Tanner said.

"Then what you're talking about are marital problems. You're wondering if your dad talked to me about such matters? Well, now that you mention it—yes. I'm sorry to say that Mack's marriage seemed to be on the rocks," Sorenson said regretfully.

Tanner was so stunned that he suddenly felt dizzy. He had no idea it was *that* bad. The pieces of the horrible puzzle were falling into place now. "Did Dad say there was another guy?" he asked, his heart racing.

"Yes," Sorenson said uncomfortably. "He called him the *homewrecker*. I forget the name he mentioned, but he did mention a name. Do you think it was the fellow your mom married?"

"Mom's new husband is Floyd Richards. Does that name ring a bell?" Tanner asked eagerly.

"Yes!" Sorenson said. "I'm sure of it. *Floyd* was the name. It was so sad. I can't imagine why any woman married to Mack would look elsewhere. But, yes, he *did* say that this guy Floyd was flirting with his wife."

"Mr. Sorenson, I'm *determined* to get justice for my dad," Tanner said, his voice shaking with emotion. "I don't know where to go from here. I could hire a private detective if he'd work cheap. Or maybe I should go to the cops with my suspicions. . . ."

Sorenson leaned forward in his chair. "Tanner, your dad meant a lot to me. He helped me launch this business. I *owe* him. That's why I'm going to help you find out the truth here. I'll get in touch with a private investigator who works for me once in a while. We use him in some of the tangled financial deals that we sometimes have to unscramble. I'll get on this right away, Tanner. Don't go to the police until I get back to you. Meantime, just stay away from this Richards guy. If he had a hand in your dad's death, you could be in danger, too," Sorenson warned.

"Yeah. I already moved out of their place. I live in a boarding house now," Tanner said.

"Good, good—just concentrate on your own life, Tanner, and I'll keep in touch. My investigator is very discreet and very thorough. If there's something rotten in Denmark, he'll find it for sure," Sorenson said confidently.

"Thanks a lot, Mr. Sorenson. My dad used to tell me he had the best boss in the world. I can sure see that," Tanner said as he shook the man's hand. Now, for the first time, Tanner felt really encouraged that justice would be done.

Mr. Sorenson was a genuine bigshot, a mover and a shaker. Guys like that got things done.

When Tanner got back to Rod's room, the phone was ringing.

"Tanner," his mother said in a strained voice, "I've been calling all over trying to find you. I finally located Rod's number. Thank God you'd written it down in the phone book. Tanner, please come over and let's talk. You've got things all wrong, son."

"I'm *not* coming over there," Tanner said flatly. "I don't ever want to be near Floyd Richards again."

"Honey, I know you don't like Floyd—but there's no reason for this terrible bitterness," Mom said.

"Mom, I know all about you and Floyd before Dad was killed, okay? It makes me sick, really sick. I'm having a real hard time even talking to *you* right now," Tanner snapped.

"Tanner, I'm telling you that you've

got it all wrong. I was *never* unfaithful to your father—never once," Mom cried.

"Drop the act, Mom. I *know*, okay? I mean there's no point in lying about it anymore. I finally understand why you were in such a hurry to marry Floyd. I always wondered how you could marry a guy you hardly knew, but you knew him *well*, didn't you?" Tanner insisted.

"Tanner, it's not true. Maybe I met Floyd in the insurance company where he worked a few times. Okay, once we had coffee while we talked about life insurance—but there was never any *relationship*! He was just a nice guy. Then, when your dad died, I guess I needed someone nice really bad, and I remembered Floyd's past kindness," Mom said. "After your father's accident, I was just so crushed, so lonely, that I needed someone. . . . "

"Dad *didn't* have an accident, Mom. He was murdered. That's another thing I'm pretty sure of now," Tanner said, almost triumphantly. "The whole rotten scheme is coming undone, Mom."

Tanner had the power now. The terrible power of truth. All these years it had been Mom, Floyd, and Damon against him. Now Tanner had the power. He knew what was going on. That was all the power he needed.

Chapter 7

"*Murdered?* Did you say your father was murdered?" Mom asked. She didn't sound as surprised as Tanner would have expected. "What makes you think such a thing?"

Tanner was horror-stricken. How could Mom be so calm? She hardly seemed shocked at all. Did she *know* what Floyd Richards had done—and married him anyway?

It was too awful to imagine! Yet her voice was frighteningly calm. It was as if she had always known that Tanner's father had been killed on purpose.

"You're not surprised, huh, Mom? Like maybe you've known all along?" Tanner asked in a savage voice. "You know what, Mom? I'm getting the truth.

Some important people are helping me. I'm gonna blow this thing wide open, Mom—and I don't care who gets burned, okay? All I know is, I'm *getting* the guy who killed Dad."

"Tanner," Mom said in a strange, trembling voice, "just leave it alone. Do you hear me? Stop now! Let sleeping dogs lie, Tanner—*I beg you!*"

"I can't let it alone," Tanner said. "It's my *father* I'm talking about. If somebody murdered him, he's gonna pay. I owe my dad some justice!"

"Tanner," Mom said, "please listen to me. *Your* own life could be in grave danger if you stir this up."

Tanner froze. Was his own mother threatening him? Was she so devoted to Floyd Richards that she was threatening her own son to spare Floyd? It seemed unbelievable.

Tanner slammed down the phone. He simply couldn't talk anymore. He couldn't contain the furious feelings that were coursing through his brain.

Tanner went for a long walk. He had to shake off the head of steam that was building up. He thought back over the last years, reliving all the times he had felt slighted by Floyd Richards. He remembered every one of them—the lesser Christmas gifts, the times Tanner didn't get to go to the baseball games when Damon did.

Tanner knew he was the kind of a person who nursed a grudge. He wasn't proud of it, but he accepted it. You could never wrong Tanner and think he would forget about it. Tanner still held a grudge against Jamie Long, the girl who turned him down for the harvest dance when he was a high school junior. Tanner's mind was like a computer that filed every slight in its memory bank and downloaded them frequently.

Eventually, Tanner ended up at the apartment where Bianca and two other girls shared expenses. Her roommates were out, but Bianca was at home. "Come on in, Tanner. I've got cheesecake and hot chocolate," she said.

Tanner went in, flopping down on Bianca's sofa. "I'm beat, babe," he said. Then he told his girlfriend everything— including his darkest suspicions. He let it all pour out. As he talked, he watched as surprise and then shock appeared on Bianca's face.

"Oh, Tanner!" Bianca cried out when he finally finished. "I just can't believe your stepdad could be such a monster. I mean, you've lived with the man ever since you were about five years old! If he was such a vicious creep to have murdered your father like that, surely you would have seen some signs of it before now!"

"Nah," Tanner said. "People can be like that. Lotta murderers are nice ordinary people on the outside. Like those Mafia guys. They got wives and kids and neighbors who swear they're great. Then one day they go out and waste a bunch of people."

"But Tanner—your *mom* would have suspected something for sure," Bianca insisted. "I mean, if she had any idea that Floyd had killed your dad, she wouldn't have married him."

"You don't understand. Mom is real gone on Floyd," Tanner said. "You should just see them together. They play around, flirting with each other like a couple of teenagers. I'm 21 and *I'd* be embarrassed to act like they do in public. It really makes me cringe sometimes. Mom is absolutely *crazy* about that fool—I think she'd forgive him for anything."

Bianca shook her head sadly. "Oh, Tanner, I feel so sorry for you. How awful it must be for you to suspect your own mom of covering up your dad's murder. I can't even imagine what you must be going through." Bianca reached over and gently massaged Tanner's neck.

"How are you going to find out for sure?"

"I got a piece of luck there, Bianca. It's this guy my dad used to work for, Mr. Sorenson. He and Dad were real good buddies. Well, I went over there and told him everything I just told you. He's getting his own private detective to look into it. He says he's got ways of getting information that I couldn't get my hands on," Tanner said enthusiastically.

"Honey," Bianca said softly, "I know it's not easy being a kid and losing your dad and then having your mom bring in a new guy to take his place. But keep your cool. You don't think all this suspicion is just resentment against your stepdad, do you? Is it possible that you've blown everything out of sight?"

"No," Tanner answered quickly. "I've already got good information that ol' Floyd was messing around with Mom behind Dad's back. And I'm convinced that the so-called accident wasn't a real accident at all. It was a hit, Bianca. I *know* it was a hit. My dad was *killed*."

"Oh, Tanner, that's so awful!" Bianca said sympathetically.

"I figure Floyd had it all arranged— even to taking the death car to some quickie paint shop. He's a real sleazy guy, always pulling sneaky stuff. I've always known he was a real lowlife," Tanner said, standing up. "Well, thanks for letting me dump on you, babe. I know this is ugly stuff. Hope I wasn't wrong to tell you. Maybe hearing about the kind of family I come from will make you want to bail out on me."

Bianca stood, too, putting her arms around Tanner. "I'd never want to bail on you, guy. I know the kind of person *you* are—and that's all I care about."

When Tanner got back to Rod's, Grandma Brice called. "Tanner, could you come over here right away? It's really important," she said.

Tanner went out to his pickup and quickly drove downtown to Grandma's apartment. Grandma was special to Tanner. When she called, he was on his way. After Dad died, Grandma's place was the only home where Tanner still felt special, where he felt totally loved. Tanner would do anything for his grandmother.

"There you are, darlin'," Grandma said when he came to the door. "Come on in. Oh, sweetie, I've been so worried about you!"

Tanner went in and sat down. "So, what's up?" he asked.

"Tanner, your mother called me. That poor woman's hysterical. She's afraid something terrible is gonna happen to you because of these old bones you're digging up!" Grandma said.

"Yeah," Tanner said bitterly, "she's afraid I'm gonna find out who killed my dad! But you lost your son, and I lost my dad. Somebody is gonna pay for that real soon. The murderer is about to be unmasked, Grandma. Mom's just afraid it's her precious Floyd Richards!"

"Oh, Tanner," Grandma cried, tears running down her cheeks, "you're *wrong*! I must tell you something now that I've never told you before. Right after Macky died, your mom was suspicious, too. She hired a private detective to get to the bottom of it. And then one night your mother got a phone call. A sinister voice said that if she didn't stop meddling in the matter, her son—*you*—might meet the same fate as Mack did."

For a moment or two Tanner was speechless with shock. "Who told you this, Grandma?" he asked, his hands tightening into fists.

"Your mother, of course," Grandma said, dabbing at her eyes.

"I figured that," Tanner said. "Maybe she was afraid you'd start digging around. She probably thought you might have doubts about Dad's death, too. Wasn't that a good way to shut the door on finding the truth? Or maybe Mom wanted to protect her precious Floyd Richards—because she *knew very well* that he had killed my dad!"

"Tanner!" Grandma cried out, "that's a *terrible* accusation. I know you've never liked Floyd. To tell you the truth, he's not one of my favorite people either. But that man is not a murderer. Lord have mercy, child—how can you even *think* such a thing?"

Chapter 8

Tanner looked directly into his grandmother's eyes. "Grandma, I love you more than I love anybody else on this crummy earth! You and my girl, Bianca, mean everything to me. You've always been there for me. But this time I gotta do *my* thing. The guy who killed Dad is not going to get away with it anymore, okay?" he said.

"Tanner, please, please let it go. I already lost a precious son. I don't want to lose you, too," Grandma Brice's voice broke and she started to cry again.

Tanner gave his grandmother a hug. "You're not gonna lose me, Grandma. I got a real powerful friend who's helping me. He's gonna get at the truth. Believe me, nobody is gonna get hurt but the creep who killed Dad!" he said.

The next day Tanner got the phone call he'd been waiting for. Dad's old boss wanted to meet him in a parking lot near the ocean. A few hours later, Tanner pulled in behind Mr. Sorenson's big sport utility vehicle.

"You got something for me, Mr. Sorenson?" Tanner asked as he sat down next to the man.

"Yes," Sorenson said grimly, "you were right in your suspicions. My man contacted another witness. Turns out this witness had a criminal record, so he made sure to slip away before the cops came. But he said your father lived long enough to say, 'Floyd got me!' Those were his exact words."

Tanner felt the inside of the cab grow dark. He was afraid he might pass out. Sure, he had had his suspicions—but it was shocking to have them so forcefully and brutally confirmed! "But, I don't understand. Why didn't the police go after Floyd Richards?" he stammered.

"Like I said, this witness had some legal problems of his own. He didn't dare show his face," Sorenson said.

"But how did your guy find him?" Tanner asked.

"The man is *good*. He's got sources on both sides of the law," Sorenson said.

"Will this guy testify so we can nail Floyd for murder?" Tanner asked.

Mr. Sorenson shook his head. "He'd never talk to the cops. He's looking at prison himself for armed robbery."

"But what am I gonna do?" Tanner cried out in frustration. "Now I know who killed my dad—but I can't do anything about it!"

Sorenson put his hand on Tanner's shoulder. "Son, I asked you to meet me out here for a good reason. I didn't want to speak frankly in my office or in any other public place. But we're totally secure here, so I can say something that is going to be very disturbing to you," he said in a low, serious tone of voice.

Tanner looked intently at the man. He was so grateful that such a clever, important man had taken up his cause. Tanner was awed by his good fortune in getting so powerful an ally. "Lay it on me, Mr. Sorenson. After all that's happened, nothing is going to shock me anymore, okay?" Tanner said.

"Well, Tanner, sometimes this is not a very nice world. We are brought up to believe that justice always triumphs in the end—but that's not always the case. I'm a realist. The truth is that a lot of innocent people get sent to the slammer—and a lot of guilty people walk. That's the long and the short of it. I've lived in this rotten world long enough to know that sometimes the only justice available is what we deal out ourselves," Sorenson said.

Tanner stared at the man, feeling thoroughly confused. "I don't get it, Mr. Sorenson."

"We know that Floyd Richards killed your father. He certainly deserves the death penalty. It was a premeditated murder, because he plotted it ahead of time to get your mother. Isn't that right, Tanner?" Sorenson asked calmly.

"Yeah, sure, but how are we gonna get him arrested and convicted? That won't happen unless this crook your guy found is willing to tell his story!" Tanner said impatiently.

"We know that's impossible. The man who witnessed the crime is now out of the country. He will never return to face the consequences of his own misdeeds. So what we have are two choices, Tanner. Either Floyd Richards gets away with murder, or you and I make sure he is punished," Sorenson said grimly.

"But I still don't get it," Tanner said.

"I loved Mack Brice like a brother. As I told you before, he joined my firm when I was a struggling beginner. It was *his* genius and loyalty that turned my company into a multimillion-dollar business. I want justice, too, Tanner. And that means we have to take things into our own hands. Think about it. Why shouldn't there be *another* accident?" Sorenson's voice sounded very calm and reasonable, softening the terrible import of his suggestion.

Tanner felt his chest turn ice cold. He couldn't believe what he was hearing. The inside of the big truck's cab seemed to be spinning around him.

Chapter 9

"*What*, Mr. Sorenson? Are you saying that *we* ought to kill Floyd Richards ourselves? Fake an accident like he did?" Tanner gasped in disbelief.

"Why not, if it's the only way?" Sorenson asked coolly.

"Wait just a minute, Mr. Sorenson! There's absolutely no way I could murder somebody!" Tanner cried.

"Not even to get justice for your dead father?" Sorenson asked in a harsh, critical voice.

"I want justice, yeah. But I'm not *killing* anybody—not even a dirtbag like Floyd Richards," Tanner said.

"I see," Sorenson sneered. "Then you only want justice when it comes easy— when the law does all the dirty work.

Well, son, it ain't gonna happen this time. If you and I don't sentence Floyd Richards to death and then carry out the sentence, your dad's murderer *walks*. I know some unsavory fellows who do that kind of work. So, if you agree with the plan, we'll make it happen. It's as simple as that."

Tanner flung open the door of the cab. "No! I want no part of this. Man, I can't believe what you're saying to me," he shouted.

"*Shhhh*," Sorenson cautioned. "Don't make a scene, Tanner. People might hear something."

"Look—let's just drop it, okay?" Tanner said nervously. "I'll keep on trying to get real evidence against Richards. Then the cops can arrest him and charge him. It's gotta be that way. I don't want anybody murdered, man! That'd make me as low as him. Let's just pretend this conversation never took place. This is just crazy!"

"So, Tanner, are you rejecting my offer to bring justice? You'd rather go to the police in a useless effort to make them reopen a 16-year-old case?" Sorenson asked with a sneer.

"Yeah, I am," Tanner said, hurrying over to his pickup truck. He felt sick to his stomach. As fast as he could, he jumped in his truck, turned over the engine, and headed home.

The next day, during his automotive classes, Tanner couldn't think of anything but the shocking offer Dad's old boss had made. So now he was right back where he started—only now it was worse. Because of the missing witness's testimony, he *knew* that Floyd Richards had killed Dad. But he couldn't do a thing about it.

Tanner was hurrying from class, racking his brain for a solution, when he almost ran into Floyd Richards.

"Tanner, wait up. I need to talk to you," the man said earnestly.

"Get away from me, man," Tanner cried out in a ferocious voice. "I got nothing to say to you."

"You think I killed your dad, don't you?" Floyd asked, "But I didn't. I hardly knew your mom when I brought her the insurance check from your father's policy. Yeah, I fell for her right away, so I started courting her. I admit that it was probably too soon. It was tacky of me— but I never had anything to do with your father's death, boy. I swear to you! *I never hurt anybody in my life!*"

"Get away from me, or so help me, I'll deck you, man!" Tanner yelled.

Floyd followed Tanner, pleading with him. "Get lost!" Tanner screamed as he headed for his pickup. It was parked in its usual place, in the student lot across the street.

Tanner never saw the car coming toward him at high speed. He'd been so lost in his own emotions that he hadn't seen the driver shadowing him earlier.

"Tanner! Look out!" Floyd shouted. Lunging at his stepson, he grabbed his sports jacket and yanked him out of the path of the speeding car. In a split second, Tanner tumbled back onto the sidewalk, stunned. His mouth was dry, his brain spinning.

Someone had tried to *kill* him—just the way his dad was killed! And Floyd Richards had saved his life.

Only this time was different. In a few minutes, the speeding car was caught, and later that day the hit man sang. *Sorenson had been behind it all.* When he had hired the hit man to kill Mack Brice, it had been a clean job. But now at last the truth was coming out.

The police discovered that Sorenson's financial advice business was just a cover for its *real* business—laundering drug money. When Mack Brice had discovered the same thing 16 years ago, Sorenson decided that he had to die— and he did.

Tanner and Bianca met for coffee that afternoon. When he had filled her in on the whole story, she smiled and said, "So your stepdad is a good guy after all, huh, Tanner?"

Tanner smiled sheepishly. "I guess *I* was the bad guy for a while there, huh? I let my jealousy of Damon poison my brain. But I'll make amends, honest I will. I'm taking the whole family out to dinner on Sunday—Mom, Damon, and my stepdad. You can meet them then, Bianca. I guess it's time. After all, they're going to be your in-laws one of these days. . . ."

Bianca grinned and kissed Tanner soundly.

COMPREHENSION QUESTIONS

RECALL

1. Why didn't Tanner want his girlfriend Bianca to meet his family?

2. How long after Mack Brice's death did Tanner's mother wait to remarry?

3. What did Bob Sorenson tell Tanner about the Brices' marriage?

4. Who did Tanner think had murdered his dad?

VOCABULARY

1. Mack Brice was Tanner's "biological" father. What does *biological* mean?

2. Tanner told himself not to be "paranoid" about Floyd Richards. What does *paranoid* mean?

3. Tanner's "makeshift" bedroom was really a small sunporch. What does *makeshift* mean?

IDENTIFYING CHARACTERS

1. Which character in the story could be described as *devious* and *ruthless*? Explain your reasoning.

2. Which character in the story became obsessed with Mack Brice's murder?

3. Which character advised Tanner to "let sleeping dogs lie"?

4. Which character told Tanner that Mack Brice had been called a *hothead*?

CAUSE AND EFFECT

1. Tanner left the family's apartment and moved in with his friend Rod. What was the *cause* of Tanner's hasty move?

2. What *effect* did Floyd Richards' line of work have on Tanner?

3. Bob Sorenson suggested a way to "bring justice" for Mack Brice's murder. What *effect* did this suggestion have on Tanner?